Arthur Loses His Marbles

A Marc Brown ARTHUR Chapter Book

Arthur Loses His Marbles

Text by Stephen Krensky
Based on a teleplay by Nick Raposo

LITTLE, BROWN AND COMPANY
New York ᠊ᢅᠣ Boston

Little, Brown and Company

Time Warner Book Group
1271 Avenue of the Americas, New York, NY 10020
Visit our Web site at www.lb-kids.com

First Edition

The characters and events portrayed in this book are fictitious.
Any similarity to real persons, living or dead, is coincidental and
not intended by the author.

Arthur® is a registered trademark of Marc Brown.

Text has been reviewed and assigned a reading level by Laurel S. Ernst,
M.A., Teachers College, Columbia University, New York, New York;
reading specialist, Chappaqua, New York.

ISBN 0-316-12711-6 (HC) / ISBN 0-316-12557-1 (PB)

10 9 8 7 6 5 4 3 2 1

WOR (hc)

COM-MO (pb)

Printed in the United States of America

To Brian Rosman

Chapter 1

• • • • • • • • • • •

Arthur, Buster, and Binky were standing on the playground when they saw Muffy coming toward them. She was lugging a big shopping bag. It looked heavy.

"Do you need any help?" Arthur called out.

"No, no," said Muffy. "I can manage." With a stubborn look on her face, she made it the last few steps. "Do you know what I have in here?"

"Something to eat?" Buster said. His stomach growled hopefully.

Muffy shook her head. "Even better."

"That's hard to believe."

"I'll show you," said Muffy. "Let's see . . . what should I show you first?" She pulled out a stack of trading cards.

"Fifty-four Dopeyman cards . . ." On the top one, a little yellow monster was surrounded by flies and a green cloud.

"Ooh!" said Binky. "You got Stinkachu! He's hard to find."

Next, Muffy pulled out a fancy toy car with a doll sitting in the front seat. "And this is the Polly Locket SUV. It has leather seats, alloy wheels, and European-style suspension."

"Life is good for Polly Locket," said Arthur.

Muffy reached into the bag a third time. "And best of all, Teeny Mimi. She sings in Italian."

"Why Italian?" asked Buster.

"Because she's from Italy," Muffy explained.

Buster nodded. If he were from Italy, he thought, he would sing in Italian, too.

"Quite a pile," said Binky.

Muffy smiled. "CDs, books, a magazine subscription, and a gift certificate to the mall. Seventeen birthday presents in all."

"But who's counting?" said Arthur.

Muffy frowned at him. "I am," she said. "Seventeen is two more than last year. I keep track so that I'll know how good a birthday it was."

"And how did this one measure up?" asked Arthur.

"Right near the top. Of course, there's no limit to how many presents you can have. But you have to be realistic, too."

Arthur smiled. "It's good you keep that in mind." He looked at her bag and noticed a strange pouch near the top of the pile.

"What's that?" he asked, pointing.

Muffy made a face as she pulled it out. "Oh, just some marbles. My cousin gave them to me. She said they're fun, but I don't see how. They don't even take batteries. I think cavemen used to play with them or something."

Arthur took out a few marbles to look at them.

"Ooh! These are great. I like the way they feel."

Buster stepped forward for a closer look. "They remind me of little planets," he said.

Arthur handed the marbles back to Muffy. "You may not think much of these, but they seem nice to me."

"Do you want them?" Muffy asked. "I know I'll never play with marbles."

"Sure," said Arthur. "Although I don't know what I'll do with them."

"You could play a game," said Binky.

"A game?"

Binky nodded. "I don't remember the name, but I know there's a game you can play with marbles. It has rules and every-thing."

"Really?" said Arthur. "That sounds like fun." He definitely wanted to find out more.

Chapter 2

• • • • • • • • • • •

The next day, Arthur and Buster found a book about marbles at the library. Then they went to the park. They drew a big circle on the ground.

"Do you think it has to be a perfect circle?" asked Buster. "This one's a little lumpy."

Arthur did not look concerned. "Don't worry," he said. "It's not as if the marbles will notice. Now, put down thirteen marbles in a cross in the middle."

"All right," said Buster. It took him a minute. "Now what?" he asked.

Arthur flipped through the book. "It says here," he said, "that the point of the game is to knock the marbles out of the ring with your *shooter*. We're going to take turns doing that."

"Which one is the shooter?" asked Buster.

"The marble that's a little bigger than the others. You start with that one in your hand." Arthur kept reading. "And then you *flick* it toward the others."

"Flick it?" asked Buster.

"You know, make it go forward. You can use your thumb or any of your other fingers."

Buster shook his hand back and forth.

"What are you doing?" asked Arthur.

"Loosening up. I don't want to pull a muscle or anything."

"Oh. It also says that the player who knocks out the most marbles wins."

"Sounds easy enough," said Buster. "Who should go first?"

"You can go," said Arthur.

"Won't that give me an advantage?" asked Buster.

Arthur smiled. "I'll get it back learning from your mistakes."

"Ah," said Buster. "Well, that's fair, I guess."

He put his shooter down, aimed, and fired it. The shooter collided with another marble, sending it rolling toward the edge of the ring.

Now it was Arthur's turn. He flicked his shooter — and sent it bouncing off a nearby tree.

"I guess I need to concentrate a little more," he said, getting up to retrieve it.

Buster fired his shooter again. This time, he knocked out two marbles at once.

"Yesss!" he shouted.

Arthur had no such luck. His next shot

came close to three marbles but missed all of them. The shot after that somehow bounced off his nose.

"This is harder than it looks," he muttered.

Buster shrugged. "I'm sure the Brain would have some complicated explanation involving angles and degrees and stuff. Me, I'm just trying to aim straight."

"So am I," said Arthur. "It's just not working out."

After a few more shots, Buster had won all the marbles.

Arthur groaned.

"Let's play again," said Buster. "Come on, I'll lend you some of my marbles."

"*Your* marbles?"

"Well, I won them, didn't I? So, should we play again?"

Arthur sighed. "I've had enough marbles for one day."

"Okay," said Buster. "I've got enough

here for a great solar system. Good game, Arthur."

He walked off with all the marbles except for the shooter Arthur was still holding.

Arthur stared at the big marble in his hand. "Maybe you really did notice the shape of the circle."

The marble said nothing in reply.

Chapter 3

• • • • • • • • • • • •

Grandma Thora was taking something hot out of her oven.

"You two are sweet to be my guinea pigs," she said to Arthur and D.W. "Not that you have to be brave about it. I think you're really going to like this."

Arthur and D.W. were sitting side by side at her kitchen table. Pal, the puppy, was lying on the floor.

"It smells, um, interesting," said Arthur.

"Very, um, interesting," said D.W.

Pal jumped up. Obviously he thought so, too.

Grandma Thora put the casserole dish

on the counter to cool. The orangey-crusty top was still bubbling.

"What's this called?" asked D.W.

Grandma Thora smiled. "I gave that considerable thought, my dear. In the end, I decided to call it tuna-roni."

"Tuna-roni," Arthur repeated slowly. "Like *tuna* and *macaroni* put together."

"Exactly. So let's load up those plates."

Grandma Thora started to reach with a big spoon, but then she stopped.

"Arthur, what's that you're fiddling with?" she asked.

Arthur held out his hand. He was holding his shooter. "Oh, this? It's my last marble."

D.W. laughed. "He lost all his other ones to Buster. Can you believe it? I could beat Buster with one hand tied behind my back."

Arthur sighed. "D.W., you only use one hand playing marbles."

"Still . . . ," said D.W.

"May I see it?" Grandma Thora asked.

Arthur handed her the shooter.

"Pretty. My taw — that's another name for a shooter — was black with red stripes. I haven't seen it in years. I wonder if I still have my marbles around here somewhere. . . ."

Arthur and D.W. looked from the bubbling tuna-roni back to their grandmother.

"Can we look for them now, Grandma?" asked Arthur.

"Please!" said D.W. "I want to see your taw!"

"Goodness. Such enthusiasm. I suppose it won't do the tuna-roni any harm to cool." She put down the spoon. "Very well, follow me."

She led the way up to the attic. Grandma Thora ignored all the old furniture and cardboard boxes. She went directly to a dusty trunk and opened the lid.

"Now, let's see," she began, rummaging around inside. "Ahhh! Here they are."

She took out a worn velvet sack.

"That's it?" said D.W.

Grandma Thora nodded. She opened the sack and poured out a few marbles.

"These sure bring back memories. This one I won from Herman Truman. And this one once belonged to the great Lefty Raposo."

"And the big one?" asked D.W.

Grandma Thora polished the marble, revealing the red streaks slashed across the black surface.

"This was my shooter, Cannonball. She almost got me to the state championship."

"Wow!" said Arthur. "You must have been a pro."

"I was really just an amateur, but I suppose I had my moments. Anyway, you can have these, Arthur. Maybe I'll come watch you play sometime."

She handed the marbles to him.

"Thanks!" he said.

He rolled Cannonball in his fingers. Was it his imagination, or did this marble seem to be pulsing with power?

He was itching to test it.

Chapter 4

• • • • • • • • • • • •

A few days later, Arthur challenged Francine to a game of marbles in the park. Buster and Muffy had come along to cheer them on. Grandma Thora was there, too, but she sat on a bench knitting a scarf while the others gathered around the ring.

The match did not go well for Arthur. After just a few minutes, there were only two shooters and one marble left in the ring. The rest were in a pile behind Francine.

Francine bent down. She aimed and shot. A miss!

Now it was Arthur's turn. His shooter, Cannonball, was all the way on the other side of the ring.

"This could be your last shot, Arthur," Buster whispered. "If you lose this, you lose everything. Don't mess it up."

Arthur bit his lip.

"Oh, yeah," Buster added. "One more thing. Stay calm."

"Excuse me," said Grandma Thora.

Arthur looked up in relief. Any delay was a help.

"I was wondering," Grandma Thora went on, "if I might take this shot for Arthur. Watching the game has brought back a lot of fond memories."

"Hmmm," said Francine. "Let me check with my sponsor."

She and Muffy whispered together for a moment.

"Okay," said Francine, "seeing as you're

a blood relative. Anything to make this game more interesting."

"Thank you, dear." Grandma Thora put away her knitting. "If you hear any creaking, pay no attention. That's just my bones putting up a mild protest."

"Take as long as you want," said Francine. "I don't want Arthur saying we didn't give you enough time."

Grandma Thora nodded. "No, we certainly wouldn't want that." She licked her finger and held it up in the air.

"What's she doing?" Buster whispered to Arthur.

"Checking the wind," he explained.

"Does that really make a difference?"

Arthur shrugged. "I don't know, but it looks very professional."

Grandma Thora seemed to be ready. She bent down, cocked her thumb, and flicked Cannonball across the circle.

It rolled smoothly to the other side —
and knocked the marble out of the circle.

"Yay!" Arthur and Buster cried together.

Grandma Thora smiled at Francine. "Just
as much fun as I remember," she said.

Francine folded her arms. She knew a
challenge when she heard one. She held
out a hand to Muffy.

"Marbles, please!"

"But, Francine, we won everything else.
It's only one —"

"I said, marbles, please." Francine
smiled at Grandma Thora. "That is, if
you'd like to play some more."

"It would be my pleasure, dear."

A short while later, Grandma Thora was
down on all fours with a huge pile of marbles beside her. There were three marbles
left in the ring. She set up Cannonball for
her next shot.

"We used to call this the atom smasher."

She made her shot. Cannonball hit all three marbles and knocked them out of the ring.

"Ouch!" said Francine, shaking her head.

"We did it, Grandma!" said Arthur, jumping for joy. "We're rich in marbles." He scooped up a big handful.

"Well," said Grandma Thora, "we would be if we were playing for 'keepsies.' Serious players only play for 'fair.'"

She divided the marbles into two equal piles and gave one pile to Francine.

"Here you go, Francine. You've got a great hook shot, but you still need more control. Try playing with your left hand sometimes."

"Thanks, Mrs. Read."

As they were getting ready to leave, Arthur decided to ask his grandmother a question.

"I was wondering . . . ," he began.

"Yes, Arthur?"

"Um, do you think you could ever teach me to play like that?"

Grandma Thora smiled at him. "I thought you'd never ask," she said.

Chapter 5

• • • • • • • • • • • •

Arthur walked onto the porch at Grandma Thora's house and opened the front door.

"Hi, Grandma! I'm here for my —"

He stopped because the house had changed. It had changed a lot. The hall was now the mouth of a cave overhung with vines.

Arthur walked inside slowly. Suddenly, red and blue glowing marbles appeared, forming a circle around him.

Arthur took out a larger white marble of his own and released it into the air. The white marble whizzed back and forth, trying to hit the red and blue marbles. But the smaller mar-

26

bles dodged out of the way. One of them hit Arthur in the nose.

"Ow!"

"Mmmm!" said Grandma Thora. She was wearing a long white robe and floating on a pillow nearby. "Talent you have. But no patience. You have much to learn."

"Arthur?"

Grandma Thora was looking at him. They were both sitting in her kitchen.

"Huh?" Arthur blinked a few times.

"I was saying, you have much to learn. Have you finished lunch?"

Arthur looked down at the tuna-roni remaining on his plate. "All done."

"Then we'd better get cracking."

"Oh, yeah. Should I set up the ring in the living room? Or do you want to go outside?"

"Goodness! It's much too early for anything like that. I have everything planned out."

"Really?" Arthur looked around. "Where do we start?"

"Follow me," she said.

Later, Arthur was back in the kitchen on his hands and knees waxing the floor. His fingers felt like lead weights. Grandma Thora had already ordered him to bang away at an old typewriter for an hour. She had also made him balance glasses of water on his hands while she talked on the phone.

"What did you say this exercise is for?" Arthur asked, panting as he scrubbed.

"Extending your reach, dear. And, of course, it's nice to see the floor get such a good cleaning."

It wasn't until the next day that they began shooting marbles. Grandma Thora started Arthur with simple shots. Then she taught him about planning ahead so that one good shot would lead to another.

Over the next week, they progressed

to tricky spins, angles, and overall game strategies.

"Always let an opponent think he's better than you," Grandma Thora explained. "That is, until you win the game."

They were outside now, staring down at a six-foot circle. Grandma Thora had set up a shot to challenge Arthur, and he was considering the best way to approach it.

"Well?" she asked.

Arthur knelt down and carefully placed his shooter. Then he flicked it sharply, knocking the marble out of the ring.

"Nice spin, Arthur. You're really getting good at this."

Arthur straightened up. "Am I ready for the championship?"

"Well, maybe not the state championship. But I'll bet you could show your friends a thing or two."

Arthur smiled. That was all he wanted to hear.

Chapter 6

· · · · · · · · · · · ·

"May I have your attention, please?"

Buster was speaking. He was standing in the park with a bunch of kids nearby. Arthur was there, and so were Fern, Binky, George, Francine, Muffy, and the Brain.

"Welcome to the first-ever Elwood City Marbles Tournament. You are all to be congratulated for having made it this far."

The Brain frowned. "But, Buster, you said no qualifications were necessary."

Buster waved away his objection. "Hey, you could have tripped and fallen on your way over here. Right now you could be in an ambulance on your way to —"

"Okay, okay," said the Brain. "Just continue."

"As I was saying," Buster went on, "this tournament will begin today with some elimination rounds."

"Tell us again about the prize," said Binky.

"Ah, yes." Buster licked his lips. "Imagine a giant ice-cream sundae. Now, double it . . . no, triple it. And that's just the beginning. There will be candy, too. Lots of candy." He held up a video camera. "I will also be chronicling the event for posterity. Years from now our devoted fans will —"

"Isn't it time to start?" Arthur whispered to him.

Buster sighed. "Some people are not as concerned about our devoted fans as I am. Very well . . . let the games begin."

Arthur and Binky played one of the first matches. Binky held his own for a while, but he slowly lost ground to Arthur's improved play. And all of the action was captured by Buster and his video camera.

"Only one marble left in the ring," Buster whispered. "The momentum has gone Arthur Read's way in the last few minutes. But fate can be fickle. He's got to hook this just right. . . ."

Arthur made his shot — and knocked Binky's marble out.

"And he does it!" said Buster. "Amazing! Arthur Read is off to a great start in this tournament. He's sent a strong message to the other competitors. Are they listening? Only time will tell."

A little later, Arthur was playing Fern.

"He's down by five," said Buster. "Arthur needs a miracle to turn this game around. Does he believe in miracles?"

Arthur shot — and managed to knock all five of Fern's marbles out of the ring.

"Yes, he does!" cried Buster. "He made the shot! Holy cow! Arthur Read has done it again."

An hour passed. More games were played, and Buster was there for them all. The one he was commenting on now had reached a critical moment.

"This shot's almost six feet away!" said Buster. "He's looking at all the angles. Should he use his forefinger or thumb? *Forefinger or thumb?*"

"Buster, would you cut that out and just take your shot?"

"Oh. Right." He handed the video camera to Muffy.

Buster bent down. "We'll go with the thumb," he said. "I've always been very attached to it."

He took his shot — and missed.

Now it was Arthur's turn. He aimed — and knocked Buster's marble out of the ring.

"And he does it!" shouted Buster. "Incredible! Arthur Read is unstoppable." He paused. "Hey, wait a minute. He just beat me! There goes my shot at the prize. No sprinkles, no chocolate-covered cherries."

"Look on the bright side," said Arthur.

"What's that?" asked Buster.

"You've recorded it all for posterity."

Chapter 7

Buster sat on a stool at the ice-cream shop, sipping a milkshake. The Brain was behind the counter. His mother was in the back room ordering supplies, so he was helping out front.

"This is a perfect shake," said Buster.

"Thanks," said the Brain.

"Do you know why it's perfect?" Buster smiled. "I'll tell you. It's because I can barely suck the milkshake up the straw. Now that's thick."

"What's thick?" asked Arthur, entering the shop.

"My milkshake. The Brain made it just right."

"Ooh," said Arthur. "Maybe I should have one, too. No, wait a minute. I can't."

"Why not?" asked Buster.

"I have to save room for that extra-special sundae I'm going to win. Just a few more players, and then . . ."

Buster made a face. "Uh, Arthur, I think you should look at the sign-up sheet."

Arthur walked over to the clipboard on the wall. "Why? Did Francine try to sign up twice? That would be . . ."

He stopped talking. He couldn't believe the name he was seeing.

"It's not possible," he said finally.

"Oh, I believe it is," said the Brain. "Walking on the ceiling may be impossible. Eating a '52 Chevy for lunch may be impossible. But this is well within the —"

"Never mind," said Arthur. "How could she? How could she do this?"

"Ah," said the Brain. "That's another question entirely."

That night, Arthur sat in his room practicing marble shots on the floor. Pal was watching him from the bed. Arthur flicked his shooter, which flew over the other marbles and hit Pal's tail.

Pal yelped at him.

"Sorry, boy. I don't know what's wrong with me. My fingers just won't do what I want them to do."

He shot again. This time, the marble ricocheted off a Bionic Bunny action figure and knocked a lamp onto the floor.

The light went out.

Arthur stared into the darkness. "I think that's a sign I should quit for tonight."

He crawled into bed with Pal beside him. "Sleep. That's all I need." He yawned. "A good night's sleep."

*   *   *

Arthur looked down. He was still in his pajamas, but he wasn't in bed. He was standing on dirt. When he looked up, the treetops were far away. How had he become this small? At that moment, three ants about Arthur's size passed, carrying a blueberry on their backs.

"Heave, ho! Heave, ho!" the ants chanted together.

"Whoa!" said Arthur. "Those are big ants. Or at least they look that way, now that I'm so small."

Suddenly, a rumbling sound filled the air. The ants looked behind them.

"Oh, no!" said one ant.

"It's coming!" said another.

"Abandon the mission. Run for your lives!"

The ants scattered in different directions. The rumbling grew louder and louder. Arthur didn't know what was making the noise until Cannonball rolled into view. It was twenty feet tall. It crushed the fallen blueberry, covering Arthur with blue juice, and continued rolling.

Arthur wiped the berry juice from his eyes and saw something on the horizon.

Arthur gasped.

Grandma Thora was following her shooter, but now she towered over him like a skyscraper.

"Sorry, dear," she said, peering down at him. "There's room for only one marbles champion in this family!"

Arthur started to run. Behind him, Cannonball had turned and was bearing down on him.

"Aiieee!" he cried.

Chapter 8

· · · · · · · · · · · ·

The final round of the first-ever Elwood City Marbles Tournament had drawn a large crowd. Almost everyone from Mr. Ratburn's class was there, but other people had stopped to watch as well.

D.W. and Mr. Read were among the spectators. They had arrived early to make sure they got a good view.

"Okay," said D.W. "Remember, we're here to root for Grandma Thora."

Mr. Read looked at her. "D.W., I am not planning to root against Arthur."

"Why not? You've known Grandma

Thora a lot longer. And besides, she's going to win. It's good to root for winners."

"I prefer to think of it differently. The Read family wins no matter what happens."

If Arthur shared this opinion, he was keeping it to himself. He was sitting on a bench a little way off, and Buster was pacing back and forth in front of him.

"Arthur, you look pale."

"I didn't sleep well," Arthur admitted.

"Well," said Buster, "sometimes sleep is overrated. Don't be nervous, Arthur. If you're nervous, your palms will sweat, and then you won't shoot right. And if you don't shoot right, you'll miss. So just calm down!"

"I am calm, Buster."

"How can you be calm?"

"Because," Arthur explained, "I know what's going to happen."

"You do?"

Arthur nodded.

"How can you know that?" Buster paused. "You don't have a crystal ball, do you?"

"No, no, but I still know what's going to happen. You see, I've decided to lose."

"What? You can't do that! Have you seen the prize? Seven types of candy, Arthur. Not five, not six . . ." — he held up seven fingers — "*Seven!* Not to mention all that ice cream. A tower of ice cream, a mountain of ice cream, a —"

"I know, I know." Arthur sighed. "But sometimes you have to think beyond your stomach. Look, if I win, Grandma Thora will be horribly embarrassed. How could I do that to my own grandmother? I mean, sure, I want to win, and I probably would. Still, I just can't hurt her. It's not right."

Buster blinked. "Gee, when you put it

like that . . . it's so nice. If I were a grand-mother, I'd want to have a grandson like you."

"So that's why losing on purpose is my only choice." He stared at Buster. "But don't tell anyone, okay? It'll be our little secret."

Buster winked and held a finger over his lips. "I'll be silent as a tomb." He looked at his watch. "Oh, it's almost time to start. I'll go make sure everything's ready." He walked off toward the crowd.

"Hey, Buster," said Binky, who was arranging the marbles in the ring. "What's up?"

Buster shook his head. "You won't believe what I just heard. . . ."

Even from a distance, Arthur smiled. It was amazing how noisy a tomb could be.

Chapter 9

• • • • • • • • • • • •

Arthur and Grandma Thora were standing on opposite sides of the ring. The marbles formed a cross in the center.

"Are you ready?" asked Buster.

Arthur and Grandma Thora bowed respectfully to each other.

"Then let's begin!" said Buster.

Arthur won the coin toss, so he went first. He bent down to take his first shot. It did not look very difficult.

"Whoops!" said Arthur, lobbing his shooter over the nearest marble.

Grandma Thora knocked out two marbles before it was Arthur's turn again.

This time he flicked his shooter right out of the ring. "Rats! Boy, am I a butterfingers today."

There was a rustling in the crowd. Binky had spread the word to his friends about Arthur's plan.

Muffy turned to Francine. "I don't care how good a grandson he is," she whispered. "This is boring!"

"I wouldn't know," said Francine. "I fell asleep five minutes ago."

Meanwhile, Grandma Thora beckoned Arthur closer for a private conference.

"Arthur," she said, "your game seems to be a little off today."

"There is a lot of pressure," he reminded her.

"True. But I have a question. Are you trying to lose on purpose?"

Arthur tried to look shocked. "Who? Me?"

His grandmother smiled at him. "Well,

you are the only other one playing the game."

"But why would I do that?"

"All right, all right," said Buster. "I hate to break this up, but we have a tournament to finish. Let's get to it."

"By all means," said Grandma Thora.

Before long, the game was almost over. Only one marble was left in the ring. The rest were in a pile next to Grandma Thora.

"Let's see," she said, walking around the edge of the circle. "This looks like a good spot to finish the game."

She bent over to place her shooter but stumbled, putting her foot in the ring.

"Oops! Oh, dear me!"

"Are you okay?" asked Arthur. "You didn't hurt yourself, did you?"

"No, no, my foot is fine." She let out a big sigh. "I wish I could say the same about the game."

"What do you mean?" Arthur asked.

"I'm disqualified," she said.

"What?" cried Arthur. "But how?"

"When I used to play," his grandmother explained, "if a player put her foot in the ring, she forfeited the game. It's a technicality, but rules are rules. So . . . you've won, Arthur."

"Really?" said Muffy.

"No way," said D.W.

"I guess that's the way the marble bounces," said Buster.

The others looked at Arthur.

Grandma Thora shook his hand, smiling. "Congratulations!"

Arthur was too stunned to say anything.

Chapter 10

• • • • • • • • • • • •

Arthur and Grandma Thora were sitting in a booth at the ice-cream shop. Between them was a giant ice-cream sundae. It had seven kinds of candy sprinkled on top and too many scoops to count.

Arthur was holding a spoon in his hand, but he wasn't doing much eating.

"How's that sundae, Arthur?" asked Grandma Thora. "Yummy?"

"No." Arthur poked at the ice cream with his spoon. "I can't enjoy it. I keep thinking back to the game. You lost on purpose, didn't you?"

"Yes. Just like you missed all those easy shots on purpose." She paused. "Now, tell the truth, Arthur. Why did you do that?"

"I don't know. I told Buster it was because I didn't want to make you look bad in front of them."

"Is that the truth?"

Arthur blushed. "No. I guess I didn't want to lose for real in front of all my friends. I mean, I could never beat you."

"How do you know? You didn't give yourself a chance. Besides, isn't it better to lose a good game than to win a bad one?"

Arthur smiled a little. "Yeah. But you know what gets me? I actually had you a couple of times."

Grandma Thora raised an eyebrow. "I beg your pardon?"

"Here, let me show you."

He plucked some of the round candies off the sundae and spread them out on the table.

"See, in the middle of the game, you left these four marbles right on the edge of the ring."

"That was all part of my plan. I was saving them for later."

"Well, I could have knocked three out with a hook shot."

"A hook shot, indeed. You'd want to use a slider in that situation."

"A slider?"

"Absolutely."

"I don't think so."

"Well, you *should* think so."

The marble talk continued long into the afternoon. The sundae, the big prize, melted quietly on the side, but neither Arthur nor Grandma Thora seemed to mind at all.